RAINFLOWERS

RAINFLOWERS

by Ann Turner
Pictures by Robert J. Blake

A Charlotte Zolotow Book

An Imprint of HarperCollins*Publishers*

For Edith,
who also loves the rain
—AT

For my sister, Barbara
—RJB

A thunderstorm swept the field

sending mice chittering
to their grass nests

sending chipmunks squeaking
to the low, stone walls

sending birds skittering
to the line of trees

sending woodchucks lumbering
to their deep, dry holes

the trees bent,
the grasses blew, all
the Queen Anne's lace flew out
like wash in a tearing wind,

the sky tumbled and rolled
with the weight of the thunder

sending horses galloping
to the edge of the woods

sending sheep scattering
to the far, thick brush

sending foxes leaping
to the piney woods

the geese rode out the storm
in the sheltering reeds.

And when the sun burst through

the rain dripped from the barn door
onto my tongue

the first chipmunks scurried
over the low, stone walls

a woodchuck stuck his head
up into the light

the horses stamped their feet
and danced like foals

and robins bloomed like flowers
in the wet, black trees.

Also by Ann Turner

Heron Street
Through Moon and Stars and Night Skies
Rosemary's Witch
Stars for Sarah

RAINFLOWERS
Text copyright © 1992 by Ann Turner
Illustrations copyright © 1992 by Robert J. Blake
Printed in the U.S.A. All rights reserved.

Library of Congress Cataloging-in-Publication Data
Turner, Ann Warren.
  Rainflowers / by Ann Turner ; pictures by Robert J. Blake.
    p.   cm.
  "A Charlotte Zolotow book."
  Summary: Animals, trees, flowers—all react to a thunderstorm and
its aftermath.
  ISBN 0-06-026041-6. — ISBN 0-06-026042-4 (lib. bdg.)
  [1. Thunderstorms—Fiction. 2. Nature—Fiction.] I. Blake,
Robert J., ill. II. Title.
PZ7.T8535Rai 1992   90-39629
[E]—dc20   CIP
                                                          AC

Typography by Anahid Hamparian
1 2 3 4 5 6 7 8 9 10
First Edition

DATE DUE

MAY 0 6 1998		
JUN 3 1998		
JUN 2 4 1998		
NOV 2 3 1998		
MAR 2 2 1999		
JUL 2 3 1999		
OCT 0 8 1999		
FEB 2 1 2003 2002		
OCT 1 7 2003		